SONG FORM 1, Ⓐ   3, Ⓑ   1, 2, 3a*, 4, Ⓐ
          2, Ⓑ   1, 2, 3*, Ⓐ   ETC.
          2, 1, Ⓐ   4, Ⓑ

OMIT "START-ED" [♪♪] WHEN GOING DIRECTLY TO Ⓐ

* USE VARIATION ON REPEATS

One Bullfrog

Written and
Illustrated
by
Sid Hausman

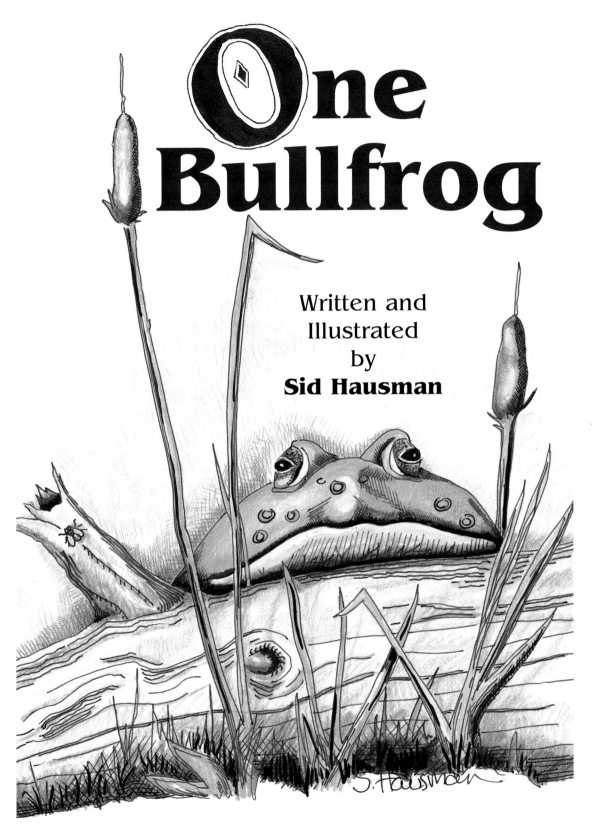

AZRO PRESS   SANTA FE, NEW MEXICO

One
Bullfrog

Text & Illustrations
COPYRIGHT © 2002 by Sid Hausman

ISBN 1-929115-05-9
Library of Congress Control Number: 2001090138

Book design by Kathleen Chambers.
The text of this book is set in Benguiat Regular 18 pt.
The illustrations are rendered in colored pencils.
Music and song written and performed by Sid Hausman.
Printed in Thailand.

Published in

Published by Azro Press   Santa Fe, New Mexico

I would like to express my appreciation to
Janice Mohr-Nelson, John Gooch and Bernard Rubenstein
for helping me transcribe the music. My thanks also to the
children at the Beklabito Day School for their enthusiasm
and creativity. I am grateful as well to my wife Cappie for
her support and assistance throughout this project.

Sid Hausman

One bullfrog sitting on a log
Over the river singing a song

Two bats started singing along
Came down to the river and sat on the log

One bullfrog

Two bats

Sitting on a log

Over the river

Singing a song

Three lizards
started singing along
Came down to the river
and sat on the log

One bullfrog

Two bats

Three lizards

Sitting on a log

Over the river

Singing a song

Four packrats
started singing along
Came down to the river
and sat on the log

One bullfrog

Two bats

Three lizards

Four packrats

Sitting on a log

Over the river

Singing a song

Five prairie dogs
started singing along
Came down to the river
and sat on the log

One bullfrog

Two bats

Three lizards

Four packrats

Five prairie dogs

Sitting on a log

Over the river

Singing a song

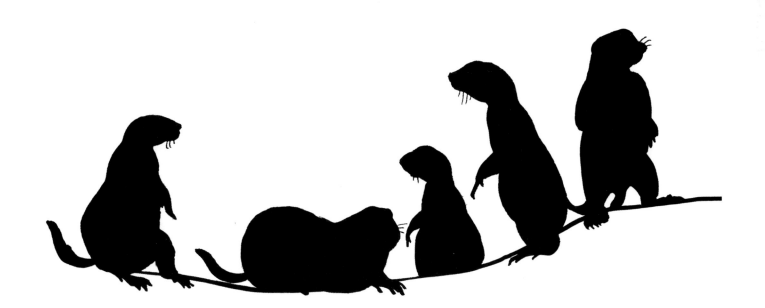

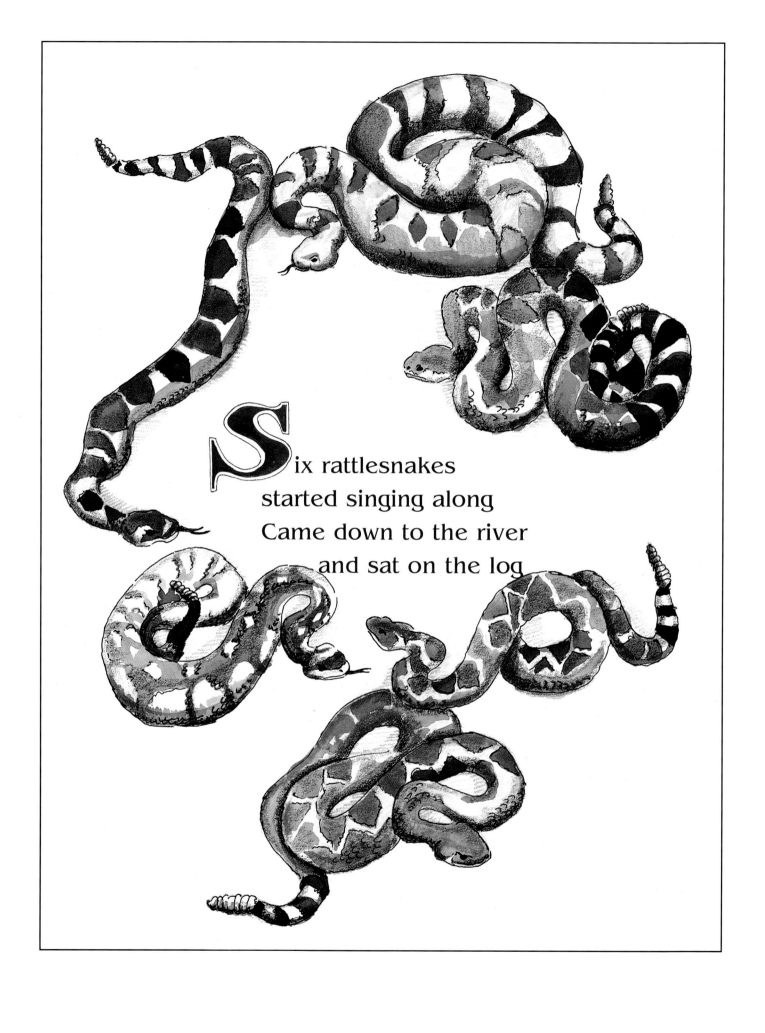

Six rattlesnakes
started singing along
Came down to the river
and sat on the log

One bullfrog

Two bats

Three lizards

Four packrats

Five prairie dogs

Six rattlesnakes

Sitting on a log

Over the river

Singing a song

Seven coyotes
started singing along
Came down to the river
and sat on the log

One bullfrog

Two bats

Three lizards

Four packrats

Five prairie dogs

Six rattlesnakes

Seven coyotes

Sitting on a log

Over the river

Singing a song

Eight bobcats
started singing along
Came down to the river
and sat on the log

One bullfrog

Two bats

Three lizards

Four packrats

Five prairie dogs

Six rattlesnakes

Seven coyotes

Eight bobcats

Sitting on a log

Over the river

Singing a song

Nine mountain lions
started singing along
Came down to the river
and sat on the log

One bullfrog

Two bats

Three lizards

Four packrats

Five prairie dogs

Six rattlesnakes

Seven coyotes

Eight bobcats

Nine mountain lions

Sitting on a log

Over the river

Singing a song

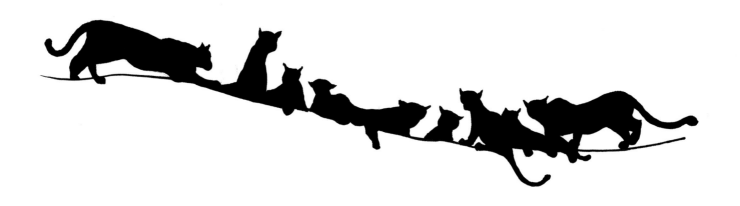

Ten bears
  started singing along
    Came down to the river
    and sat on the log

One bullfrog

Two bats

Three lizards

Four packrats

Five prairie dogs

Six rattlesnakes

Seven coyotes

Eight bobcats

Nine mountain lions

Ten bears

Sitting on a log

Over the river

Singing a song

But the log broke

and they all splashed around

In the middle of the river

when the bears sat down

Glossary

Bullfrog: Found throughout the United States, the bullfrog is the largest of our frogs. They are usually drab green and can be heard croaking in swamps and ponds at all hours of the day.

Bats: Primarily nocturnal, bats can be found throughout the southwest. Bats are a great asset in mosquito control as they eat a huge number of insects during a night out. Usually found around streams and rivers, bats live in cave-like structures during the day. They communicate with each other using sonar.

Lizards: The three lizards shown in this book are a chuckwalla, a gecko, and a skink.

Chuckwallas are one of the largest lizards in the country. They feed on cactus buds and flowers. When frightened, chuckwallas will often crawl under a rock or crevice and inflate themselves with air.

Geckos are some of the smaller lizards found in the extreme southern areas of the west. They have tiny suction cups on their toes enabling them to walk on ceilings and other vertical places. Some species also make a chirping sound that resembles singing.

Skinks are sleek, glossy lizards that have very small legs yet are extremely fast runners. Skinks live mostly on insects and small vertebrates and are found throughout North America.

Packrats: Packrats are collectors. Often their homes, found in deserted sheds or under rocks, are filled with treasures such as lost earrings, pieces of glass and other shiny things. These dens are often lined with cholla cactus making it a sticky job retrieving any of their loot.

Prairie Dogs: Living in colonies, these social little critters have become quite newsworthy lately. Property owners want them off their land but as it turns out, they are very important to the health of the open land. Their burrows aerate the soil and their seed eating spreads plant varieties around. They have a very highly developed communication system and can actually describe individual predators, reacting differently to different threats.

Rattlesnakes: Rattlesnakes, possessing a noticeably triangular head, are typically American snakes, found nowhere else in the world. They are the only snakes that warn trespassers of their presence by vibrating their tails. They are also known as pit vipers because of the heat sensitivity depression in their nose. Rattlesnakes bear live young and are generally not aggressive unless cornered.

Coyotes: The coyote, once a western species, is now found in almost every state due to his adaptability. In the Navajo culture the coyote is known as both the trickster and the sage. The Navajos feel that in the end the cockroach and the coyote will be the last survivors. Once known to early Western settlers as a prairie wolf, the coyote loves to serenade the mesas and grasslands with moonlight songs.

Bobcats: The bobcat is native only to North America and has been called the "phantom of the forest." When caught in the open, they give the appearance of having no fear; they don't run off but rather walk away seemingly unconcerned. Bobcats will make a lair in a cave and give birth to 3 to 4 kittens in the spring.

Mountain Lions: The largest cat in the United States, mountain lions are known by several names including cougar, puma, panther and catamount. Unlike lions and tigers, the mountain lion does not roar but can purr. Their habitat tends to be high rugged country but because of development, they have been seen more and more in urban areas. Mountain lions are territorial and naturally limit their own numbers by litter size. Their territory is determined by the available food supply.

Bears: Navajos feel they are distantly related to bears and treat them with reverence. Bears have almost a human like quality at times, walking on two legs and sitting on their haunches. Often called "nature's clowns," bears are omnivores and have a taste for nearly everything. In the northwest, parks post warning signs telling campers not to leave anything with an odor in the tent at night in order to avoid attack. Because of their size, adult bears have few enemies except humans.

ONE BULLFROG was written during my residency at the Beklabito Day School on the Navajo reservation near Shiprock, New Mexico. The first graders wanted to write a song about animals so I asked them to each choose their favorite one from the area where they lived. The animals were written down on a blackboard and then organized by size. We decided to see how many we could get on a log and came up with more than fifty before the log broke. Aside from being a fun project, **ONE BULLFROG** has become one of my most requested children's songs.

Sid Hausman

Photo by Roger Baker

Sid Hausman has lived in New Mexico for more than 35 years. An illustrator and western music performer, Sid has been a resident artist with the New Mexico Arts Division teaching songwriting at museums and Navajo, pueblo, and public schools. He currently gives workshops throughout the west and will usually have the kids illustrate their visual interpretations of the songs they write.